Handwritten Letters to the Devil

Experienced by

Captain Aaron Kaes and ZiN

Created by

The Lady BellaDonna, Captain
Aaron Kaes, and ZiN

Handwritten Letters to the Devil
Copyright © 2013 by ZiN, The Lady Belladona, Captain Kaes. All Rights Reserved.
Internal Graphics Design Copyright © 2013 by ZiN, The Lady Belladona, Captain Kaes.
All Rights Reserved.

PUBLISHER:
Zaloli Media Entertainment, LLC Colorado Springs, CO 80904
Toll Free: (877) 495-5836
Email: info@zaloli.com

© Copyright 2013 – Zaloli Media Entertainment. Library of Congress Cataloging-in-Publication Data

ISBN Paper Back: 978-0-9857047-6-6

ISBN Hard Back: 978-0-9857047-4-2

ISBN Electronic: 978-0-9857047-9-7

Cover Design & Layout:
GoldFlagStudios, a ZMe Production Company

All rights reserved, including the right to reproduce this book, or portions thereof, in any form.

Ingram Book Distribution for eBook: Ingram Book Company
One Ingram Blvd.
La Vergne, TN 37086

Print-on-demand Hard & Soft copy: Lightning Source Inc.
1246 Heil Quaker Blvd.
La Vergne, TN 37086

Table of Contents

1. Fate

2. Love's Last Breath

3. Patient 604

4. With God's Grace

5. Eyes of the Ghost

6. Picasso Understands

7. True Love

8. The Fire of 1922

9. Dark Blue

10. Morty-fied

11. Secrets of SaMLanD

12. My Spider's Web

13. A Hand-Written Letter

14. Cheers of the Damned

15. Oh Doctor

16. My Heart HeartHeart

17. Journal Entry 1 of 3

18. 8 Legs 6 Feet

19. Love Never Screams

20. Eating for Two

21. Sh...Sh...IREN

(Dedications)

Dedications from ZiN

To those who thought of me as unintelligent. To those who thought I could never be a writer. I'm an author now!

Dedications from Captain Aaron S. Kaes

To Mila Joe

Dedications from The Lady BellaDonna

For those that hesitate to make their own dreams come true... follow your own path and believe in yourself-make it happen.

(Beginning Quotes)

"I weep for you humanity, not for the things you have done, but for the things you could have done."

-Captain Aaron S. Kaes-

"Dude, you can't quit. It's the Army. I don't think they let you do that."

-ZiN-

"The flames of life are yours to control, breath in deep and watch them grow."

-The Lady BellaDonna-

Fate

I did not write this. You will never know who I am. I am simply the messenger.

I wish I wouldn't have walked in there. I wish I wouldn't have been drawn to that side of the room. I wish I wouldn't have seen that piano. I can almost blame my parents for pushing me so hard into music. Or the antique store for not going through their merchandise before selling it. If only someone else had seen that piano before me. If only that piano wasn't meant for me. If only what was inside, wasn't meant for me to find.

It was a 1920's player piano, and in bad shape at that. All the parts were there, but it was rough. But rough in a good way. The sound was good but out of tune, and there were some dead notes. I liked it immediately. A six pack for each of my friends secured it to my house, but it was up to me and me alone to bring this monster back to life.

I started with the pedals, which only needed to be reattached. Then the shelving was removed and refinished. Next the missing keys actually replaced with some cheap vinyl. Then, while trying to find out the cause for the dead notes, I found it. It was an old stained manila envelope. It had no markings what so ever, and looked like it had never been opened. I carefully pulled it out of the cavity, and turned it over in my hands. It felt thick, like there were a hundred or so pages that had been fused all together. I opened it carefully while secretly hoping for stacks of money to fall out of it, but only loose leaf paper did. The paper had writing on it, but most of it is so faded that you couldn't make out what it said. I spent three days reading what I could and gathered all the papers together. It was unbelievable. It seemed to be a collection of confessions to hideous crimes committed throughout the years, although I couldn't determine if it was one person or a group of confessors.

I went back to the antique store to get more information on where this piano came from and they only said up North somewhere. No luck there considering North is a big area to be from. I then went home and went over every inch of the piano. In the same place where I found the envelope, I found burned into the wood in small printing press letters,

I submit to you

These handwritten letters to the Devil

Meant to be and meant for you

As cities burn and cities level...

A chill ran through me as I read those words for the first time. What the hell did I buy? I took the letters to the police next, but the inconsistency and authentication of the pages was questioned. It was clear that a crazy person wrote these, or a group of crazies, but what they didn't seem to understand was that just because it was crazy didn't mean that it didn't actually happen.

I did some investigating on my own and found that some of the dates actually matched up to some of the crimes committed. It became weirder and weirder the more I got involved, but the police seemed uninterested. Finally, I guess I was just compelled to get these stories heard so maybe some public outcry can motivate the police to get off of their asses and look into this legitimate lead, so I published the pages under the title that was burned into the inside of my piano, and here you are. And here are "The Handwritten Letters to the Devil" in the exact order that I read them in. I'm not sure if they are connected, or if they are even real. I will leave that up to you to decide for yourself.

Love's Last Breath

She screamed. Oh, did she scream. She screamed like her last breath meant nothing to her. She belted out everything she had, without a care, or thought, or even an understanding of what it meant to me. Of how her last moments would stay with me forever.Like I wanted to remember her that way.Selfish bitch. When her eyes broke their veins like neon fault lines of color and despair, she looked at me. Looked through me. She saw who I really was for the first time, and I smiled.

    I met her in September. She was skinny, tall, and dressed in black. Yet somehow tasteful, and respectful. The first thing I noticed about her was her laugh. It seemed to make molecules themselves dance. I yearned for it. I required it. And it was mine.

    Our first date was a walk. Low commitment was a mutual thing. We walked, and she laughed, and I soaked it in like rays from the sun. I used to boast I could survive that way, like some sort of photosynthetic monster. Little did she know.

    We made love, and grew close. Everyday new admissions, and every day I grew to love her more. I hated to see her sad. It killed me. I grew to depend on her spirit to lift me up, and when she couldn't, I would starve.

    She had friends and family, of course they had to go. Little by little they began to disappear. Everybody that tried to steal her away from me ended up missing. It started with her cat. Always on her lap, always demanding affection. Always taking what was rightfully mine. It had an accident with the front and rear tires of my car. Yet somehow when I curled up in her lap and told her the cat was dead, she didn't laugh. I felt hurt. I wasn't a better substitute than her cat? She had no sympathy for my feelings.

    Next, Monday night with her parents

became Tuesday morning at the police station. Her best friends began to ignore her calls. Then her nosey know it all sister caught on to me. At this point the bodies were really stacking up and they were hard to hide. In hindsight, the iced over swimming pool was not a very good hiding spot. She had to go.

    You would think that with all the holes in her life, that she would cling to me. She would be drawn to me more often, but she became secluded, and I hungered for her. Then it happened. She told me that with all of her family disappearing that she wanted to move away. That she was breaking up with me. She actually told me that she feared for her safety. Like I would let somebody hurt her. I took offense. I kissed her gently, and then asked her to laugh for me. She just stared. Can you believe it? Just stared at me. With one hand, I slid down her cheek and pinched the end of her chin. I told her to laugh, and she began to cry, and as my hands slid to her throat and her body to the floor, she began to scream.

    I wish I could say that this is my only confession. But like God is to wine, so am I to steam, and this little engine did what it could. The following pages are all my confessions, and I ask you not to judge me, for I will be the one by which all others are judged.

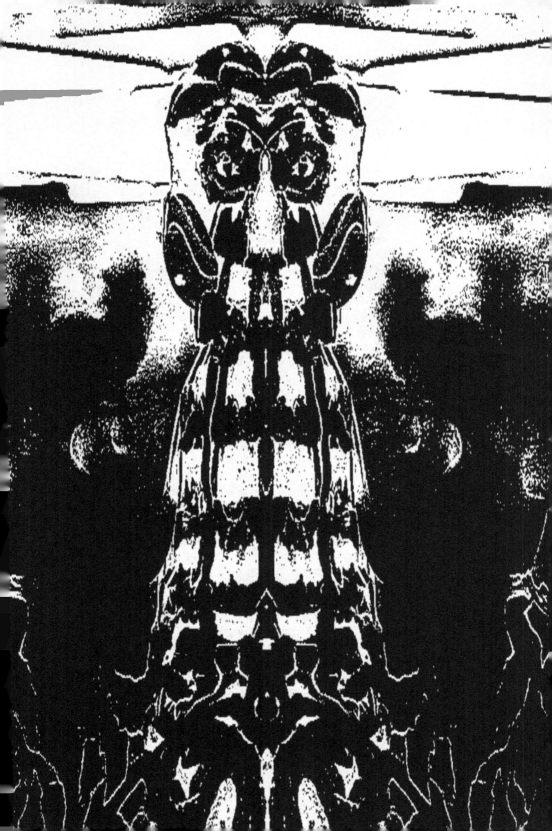

Patient 604: James William Colace

(Self given Nickname, "Silly Willy")

      Psychiatric log; day 1 of patient 604, James Colace. Our appointment was scheduled for 9:00 am on September 26, 2013. I arrived as I always do in the morning at 7:45 am to prepare for the days work and be ready by 8:00 am sharp. I spent the first fifteen minutes readying coffee, tea, and candies for my patients. This calms my patients subtly if need be during our conversations and therapy if our sessions grow too intense. I spent the next forty-five minutes reviewing the court delivered file on patient 604. His file was like many others I have seen across my desk; acute obsessive compulsive disorder, extreme bi-polar disorder, borderline personality disorder, insomnia, depression, alcohol disorder, de-realization disorder, OCPD, morbid jealousy disorder...etc. The list went on. There was no reason to continue counting disorders. Issues like this are only started by dramatic effects on ones childhood. Given James Colace was born March 27, 1987 makes him only 26. If I am to aid him in any form or fashion I need to reach the route of his issues: when they started, why they started, his perception of the events that transpired...etc. The file also showed all of the patient's previous physiatrists, there were eleven. Many prescribed drugs but none were found in James' blood work or hair follicles.

      The second file was one of dismay, his conviction file; six accounts of assault and battery, three of which were police officers, two of which were women in their thirties, and one male body builder. Also in the file were DUI and DWI charges. His license has been revoked, and is suspect in twenty-six missing person cases. Also, there are several accounts of animal cruelty.

At 8:45 am there was a sharp knock on my office door. "Come in" I said as I cleared my throat. Two officers walked in proficiently, one stayed at the door and the other walked right up to my desk and extended his hand.

"Officer Drake here with your 9:00 appointment Doc."

He was a large man, early thirties I would guess, clean shaven face, squinty eyes and cut jaw, looked ex-military if you ask me. I stood and took his hand.

"Thank you for being early, I trust you found my office ok?"

"Yes sir, no problems what so ever, are you ready for him then?"

I smiled politely and nodded, "I am thank you."

With that he turned on a dime and walked to the door, and shouted "Alright Spense bring him in." An officer came through the door dragging a man wearing handcuffs and what looked like white pajamas. He looked just like any normal man would, excluding the handcuffs and PJ's. He looked at me, and then to the chair in front of my desk, then to the officer dragging him, then back to me. I smiled my sympathetic smile.

"Welcome to my office James, I'm Doctor Gerald Godfree." I extended my hand. He mustered a half smile and raised his bound hands and accepted my gesture of introduction...so far off to a better start than most of my patients if I might add. I motioned to the chair next to him. "Please make yourself as comfortable as you can, given the circumstances."

He sat carefully examining my desk and the chair, after sitting he raised his restraints and looked at the officer. Without a moments pause, the officer produced shackles and bound him to the chair. Making sure he cuffed his feet, also his arms behind the chair back, and then stood next to him.

Officer Drake then spoke, "Alright Doc we are right outside the door if you need us. Don't hesitate for a moment to call."

I could feel my shocked expression and tried to compose myself. "Of course officer, thank you for your time." The officers left and we were alone. The blank expression on Mr. Colace's face was one of repetition. He had been in a chair like this many times before and was going through the motions. I attempted conversation.

"Do you mind if I call you James or do you prefer a different name?"

His eyes never left mine as a bright smile appeared across his face.

"I prefer Willy, but what ever makes you comfortable to call me, you may."

I smiled, "Very well Willy, would you like coffee or tea? Or water perhaps?"

He answered very politely, "Tea would be great. I've been craving it for days, thank you."

I got him tea and coffee for me, he tasted it and nodded with approval. "Thank you doctor, it is excellent."

We sat in silence as we both took sips from our beverages. We made eye contact and smiled, he was the first to speak.

"So, Doctor, what made you seek a profession aiding mentally injured individuals, I mean no disrespect by this question, I actually am very grateful that you have sought this profession. I hope to be able to one day be rehabilitated into society completely cured of my disorders," he chuckled a little, "or at least have them managed."

I smiled and dipped my head in sort of a half nod. "Well, forgetting the fact that I enjoy helping people and seeing them get better. I sometimes can find new disorders and issues in a troubled mind. I can use my research to help cure hundreds of other people suffering from the same new symptoms around the world. The more help I can do, I will always try to do."

His expression changed to one of endearing, as if I could see respect for me in his eyes.

"Doctor I believe that is the best answer I have ever received from a shrink." He said. We both shared a laugh. He seemed to ease up even more, he began massaging his hands in his cuffs. I have noticed this kind of behavior with several other of my patients. When they begin to accept someone into their lives they tend to notice physical pain more and subtly treat it as if to feel more comfortable with their current environment... it's a good thing.

I couldn't help noticing that he was showing no signs of violence or depression or any kind of hostility for that matter. The man I was sitting across from seemed to want to be a better person. Perhaps if I played my cards right I could honestly help him. I decided to switch to the defensive to see a reaction. "So, what are you hoping to accomplish by meeting with me, what goals should we make together to further you on the road to rehabilitation?"

He laughed a charming laugh, nodded his head several times, "Goals..." he said. "Goals are very important in life." He kept nodding over and over looking at my desk. After several moments of silence, he spoke the words that would make me realize the severity of his condition.

"We have all the time in the world for goals, Gerald, but right now we should worry about the safety of your children and your ex-wife. I fear, the most ghostly of fears, a demented psychopathic serial murder is soon on his way to their home in the suburbs driving your vehicle."

Fear washed over me as he finished speaking, I could feel my mouth hanging at his last word. My voice came in a whisper.

"Why would you think that?"

His eyes never left mine as he raised his unbound hands and smiled a smile I could never forget.

With God's Grace

       Father Thompson came forward from the darkness to the third pew where he always sat. He prayed there every Sunday for the last three months or so. The face we have all accepted as one of ours. A handsome man full of life and a love for all that is created. Always showing trust in everyone who would walk through our church doors. His smile is so warming to our hearts. That man must have been an angel in his past lives. Father Thompson sat next to him in the pew and put a hand on his shoulder.

"It is always good to see you my son. How has your last week been?"

The bright and lively smile leapt to his face at the sight of the father.

"Oh Father I have had the loveliest week of my life, I have fallen in love with someone. This person, Father, is lovelier that a thousand roses freshly bloomed on a spring day in heaven."

The Father laughed with delight.

"Oh that is wonderful news! Love is God's sunshine beaming down to mankind to remind them of his glory. Tell me my son, what is your love's name?"

He beamed with delight, "Athena, Athena my own human love."

The Father bowed slightly, "That is a lovely name, most fitting for a lovely woman."

The young man looked down at the floor still smiling. "Yes, it is most fitting for a most lovely person in the world." Several moments went by when he finally came back down to our earth. "Well father, I would like to have my weekly confession, do you have time for me today?"

Father Thompson broke into smiling laughter. "Of course my son, for you I will always have time. They both headed towards the confession booth.

It was a little less than half an hour when Sister Brooke called the police. Officer Tain was first on the scene. Sister Brooke was sobbing and being consoled by a number of other Sisters, also crying. A crowd had gathered in the congregation hall around the confession booth. Officer Tain pushed his way through the crowd. "Alright everyone, BPD, everyone BACK UP!" The crowd moved enough for him to get to the booth and look at the scene. The sight of the deceased instantly induced vomit.

In the detectives report, Father Thompson's body was found in the confession booth with out pants, on all fours. Eyes gauged bluntly, most likely with thumbs, the other side of the confession booth that was separated by a flimsy wooden barrier was broken. The anus of the father was soaked with blood, and semen was found in the cavity, obvious rape. The killer had scratched these words in the back of the victim, possibly with fingernails: "Athena, why defy me."

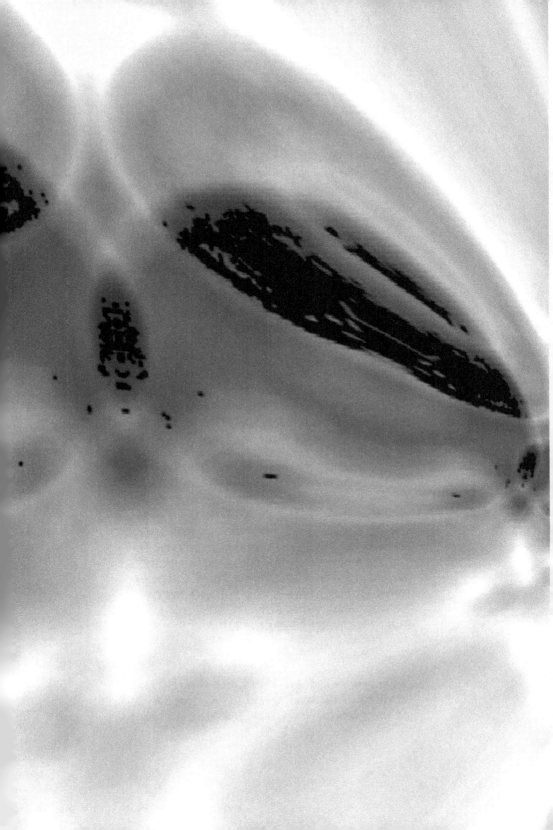

Eyes of the Ghost

"It's only fitting that I am the one who keeps you safe. No one is what I am, no one is how I am. I can remember how you wished for help, begged for protection. Seeing your tears was more than I could ever bear. No one will harm you. No one will judge you, say you can't do anything. You will fly, soar like airplanes, like angels, like the most powerful God. With me here for you, living for you, being your tank.

Here comes the rain, but you won't feel it. I will take the brunt of it. You will always be warm, dry, safe. In this blackness I stand in now, you will see light, because I can see in the dark. I can bask in blackness and see our future. Seeing you in my box, in my sight, in my hand. You love me, I can hear you beg for me through this glass. You know you need me, I'll show you that you're right. I could look at you for eight life times, never moving. I would lay in your aurora and starve if it made you happy.

My hoody is soaked now but I'm happy you are dreaming of me. Hearing your moan, I know it's for me. You are starting to rustle now. When I see your body move like that you know what it does to me. You tease. You slut. You whore. Why are you torturing me, you know I'm here to protect you. Stop begging for me. I want you too. I need you too. YOU WHORE! STOP HURTING ME! YOU'LL BE SORRY! ILL SHOW YOU! IM GOING TO GET YOU! NO ONE CAN PROTECT YOU! YOU'RE GOING TO SWALLOW IT! I SWEAR YOU WILL! YOU'RE MINE!"

"You're awake..."

She shot up in bed. Sweat streamed down her face. The rain was slamming against the window, the darkness was so thick outside. She swore she heard someone yelling but it was probably just the storm outside.

A flash of lightning shows blackened eyes in her window.

She screams and produces a pistol and runs to the window. Nobody there. She sighs relief. It was just the tree next to her window. Back to sleep.

The moment sleep takes her back, the Eye of the Ghost returns...

<u>Picasso Understands</u>

She looked into my eyes, saw the blood on my face, and began to cry. She was 6 years old, and recently an orphan thanks to yours truly. There are so many places to hide in a hotel room. I would have never found her except for the sniffling. When I put the gun next to her face she stopped crying. I told her to look at her parents, who were answering role call naked and dead on the stained 1980's carpet, and when she did I saw her eyes break. She would never be the same.

There was an old movie playing on the TV when I came in disguised as room service. Apparently the villain and I were both feeling very cliché that day. He had a sinister mustache and had tied somebody to some train tracks. I just had a silencer and some chloroform. I made the parents breathe deep, then stripped them down, then shot them directly in the face. That is when I heard noises from the closet. She said the bad man from the TV had scared her. I said she didn't know fear yet. I told her that I would teach her. I hit her as hard as I could over the head with the gun and she fell to the ground. Her bowels released and a mixture of bodily fluids started to pool around her in alphabetical order. I imagined her singing her ABC's as the blood started to flood my feet.

I quickly took her to the bathroom where I ran a hot bath. I placed her in the tub face up and went to the mirror, which was beginning to fog up. Her father's straight razor was sitting by the sink and I instinctually picked it up and ran it over my chest. I had done this a thousand times before, and every time the same thing happened. I didn't even feel the blade, but the blood was warm and familiar. When I looked down though, there wasn't any blood. Just a big tear in my shirt. I took the razor to my forehead next. Not even a scratch. Had I finally done it? Was I invincible? She began to stir and sob like a lost puppy, and as I turned to her, my face cut to ribbons, her cries turned to screams and I knew that she shouldn't have made me feel so insecure.

I black out, and when I come to, her head as been shaved as well as part of one eyebrow. I was driving an unfamiliar car, and there were some crudely drawn plans on the dash. I couldn't believe what I saw. These ideas were amazing! Did I really come up with them? I took a look in the rearview just to make sure that it was actually me in the reflection. The man staring back at me had glued the girl's hair to my face in the shape of a mustache. I really kind of liked it. It made me feel dangerous. It made me feel secure.

I worked all afternoon. Digging, sawing, and tying were the songs in my head, and I had an obsession. This was going to be my masterpiece, and I had that old movie to thank.

I asked my lovely assistant if she was ready and she started whispering something I couldn't quite make out. It turns out that when you strip a little girl naked and tie her to some railroad tracks in the hot sun for hours, she gets thirsty. I went back to the car and moved my copy of the train schedule to get to a juice box that had been in the car for god knows how long. As I strolled back to her, sipping on the fruit punch, I heard it. Faint at first, but getting louder. I felt a slight tremor in my boots and I knew that my hard work was going to come to fruition. I kneeled over her and gave her the rest of her juice. I asked her if she was scared and she just nodded. I said good and got into position. I had the perfect spot picked out, and it was all going according to plan. I wouldn't miss a thing. Her body hovered 50 ft above the river, and the train was barreling towards us. I smiled and felt good in my decision to tie her to tracks on a bridge.

The train horn made my heart race like locomotion itself. The black coal of my heart fueling my hate like a beautiful machine designed to do one thing and do it well. She began to scream as the train drew near, and I believed her fear. Even now it brings chills to my arms to remember how honest she was in those last moments, how terror really felt, what it feels like to have your worst fear come true.

As the train made its way to its final stop at destination little girl, I pulled the rope, releasing the pin and hinges that I had installed to the tracks and a three ft. section broke free. There was an immeasurable amount of silence as she fell from the bridge. She was still tied to the section of free falling track, plus a very fashionable necklace of my own design, when it suddenly stopped twenty feet above the water. The noose did not break her neck so I stood there watching her silhouette hang naked beneath a train in the sunset. She kicked and squirmed, but it didn't take long. I didn't cut her down. Would you ask Picasso to not hang is artwork?

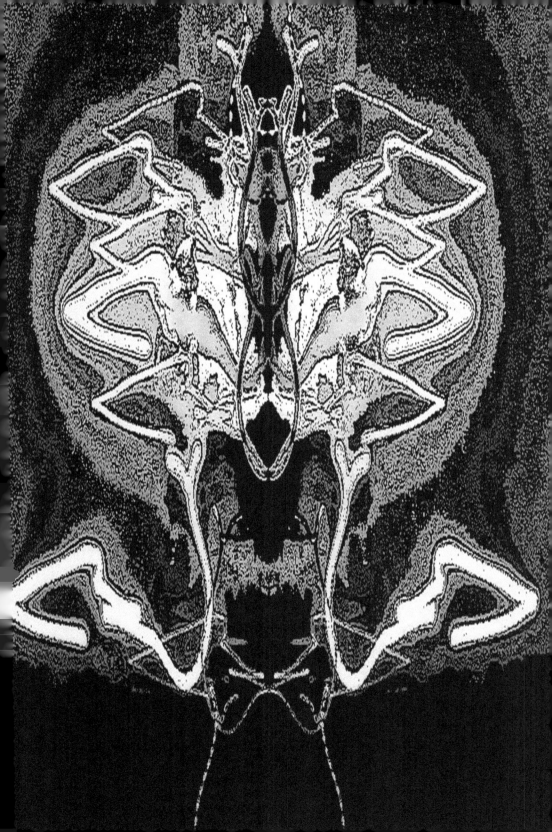

True Love

We have been together for eight months, twelve days, seven hours, and fifty-two minutes...but who's counting!? We have a Special Date tonight and I'm beside myself I'm so excited. He is taking me out to a lovely steak and lobster dinner at Nikkita's. Red wine, dim lighting, candle on the table to set the mood, jazz playing in the background as we stare into each other eyes. Of course I'll have on my skinny black dress and heels to match, my hair curled in an updo with smokey eyes and ruby red lips to complete the ensemble. I know he will be dressed to the nine's as well, slick pants, shiny belt and shoes, button down shirt and a suit jacket, smelling like only he can with a grin to die for. Supposedly after dinner there is a surprise for me having to do with stars and city lights in a romantic old fashioned way...of course he doesn't know what a surprise I have in store for him tonight.

What a wonderful night! I love this man! An amazing dinner full of savory flavor and looks of adoration, followed by a cuddled, romantic, horse drawn carriage through the city. Of course the seduction didn't stop there...we came back to my place for more wine, and dessert. Dessert, of course, being a sweet love making session with passionate kisses and caresses that leave you tingling and euphoric. Just the things all romantic movies are made of. All the things that every girl dreams of having, a fairy tale of awe. Every girl that is, except me. While I can say it is refreshing to have a break from the regular humdrum of this boring life, I much prefer a different affection. A more macabre look into lust...and the dizzying stumbles and vacant look on his face tell me it is almost show time.

"Excuse me my dearest; I must go powder my nose. Don't go anywhere...I'll be back at my soonest"

Shed this lie I'm living, remove this makeup and fifties way of life from my temple. Time for something more... comfortable. Black vinyl and leather, straps and buckles for him. Bustles, garters, and fine satin for me. Victorian royalty meets the sirens of Hell's gates. The elegance of ruffles and lace offset by his studs and chains. A truer match could ne'er be found. On second thought...tonight is supposed to be special. Hmmm. Instead of leather and hooks and bondage, I think a more simplistic approach is required. He will be in his truest form, the one that cannot lie. Naked and roped so as to keep him awake.

"I told you I'd return, my love," I lift his chin so that he may gaze upon my beauty as I speak to him. His eyes are mostly vacant from the wine and Flunitrazepam that laced his glass.

"Fret not, my dearest, I will bring back the light to your eyes."

Now for my favorite part; time to pick the tools that help our love grow...the tools that will help release his essence and prove that this is not a movie or charade of sorts. The tools... - which oddly enough - are not where I placed them. Oh what a sneaky minx he is, or so he thinks. We shall see who the minx is, and who the mouse is.

Small, teasing whips from my riding crop should help rectify this little dilemma. Sliding the whip across his body as I circle him like a raven in the night, every so often giving a little crack to ensure he is paying attention to my every syllable. His head bobs with every flash of leather on skin, a reaction I need more of. I give a good crack to his inner left thigh, high enough to hit the sensitive area, just shy of being cruel. He groans- a noise that fills me up like helium in a hot air balloon. My urge gets stronger. My need for his love growing. As if on it's own accord, my whip finds it's way between his quivering legs and raises my lie detector for a better inspection. I take control, gripping firmly around the base of the crown jewels and giving a slight tug for assurance.

"Do you love me?"

His head bobbles with a grunt. Not good enough. I give a firm slap of my whip, to which I get a much more satisfactory reaction. His head slams back with a groan. Mmm, that's better.

"You do love me, don't you?"

A bobble-headed response...again not good enough. Time to get more romantic. Perhaps some foreplay to warm him up out of the drugged haze. The feel of his skin under my nails is enticing. The red marks left behind please me. They only show up for me. My teeth sink into his flesh as he groans and wriggles. His scent is becoming mine as well. I yearn to see if he is being truthful to me. He is indeed. His sword is immaculate. Strong and steady as if ready for battle, ready to pierce the very source of any oncoming attack. This pleases me, so much so that I indulge myself a little. I must sheath this sword, as it is not time yet for battle. And what better protection than that of mine own tongue and lips. But wait...I am not dressed for such an occasion. A dagger from my garter helps me cure my distress. A sweet slice of his wrist, a delicate caress of the steel on his paper-thin skin lets my love run rampant. The crimson tide that stole my heart reins supreme once more. I flitter with desire. He moans and I know. I know he is mine. I can help myself no longer; a shaking hand leads me to the source. I must remain in control. I mustn't give in to temptation too soon. But I cannot help myself. It calls to me, glistening in the candlelight. I must feel its warmth. I must have it. My finger gathers this miraculous love and spreads its joy on mine lips so that I may feel and taste and be of him. Now the sheath is complete, decorated to its best so that it may cover the sword in all its glory till the battle begins. Oh and what a glorious decoration it is. But now it is time. It is the hour of the battle. I must prepare.

Taking my dagger, I release his ropes. He falls to the cushions I have left for him with a sigh.

"It's your turn now. Your turn to have me prove my love to you"

I force the sword into his hand and his head to my bosom. He kisses just where my dress meets my skin, tantalizing me. He takes the blade, and with an exasperated grunt forces it into me. Penetrating my being. But the battle has nearly begun, and his forces grow stronger than my own. I reach for the dagger that I left on the floor; his hand on my wrist just as I reach the handle. He lifts his head and looks straight into my eyes as he turns the dagger onto me. The place he had been kissing was now his strategic upturn of the battle. The cold of the metal and the warmth of my love creating their own unending vows. A razor from my breast soon proves to stabilize this war. With one swift caress his love rains down on me. I can feel his warmth and energy. That which cannot be denied. It cannot be taken back. It is mine. Our love intertwines as our bodies beat in unison. Cut to cut we become one. I bathe in it, ensuring every inch of me is covered in his love and in turn, ensuring he is covered in mine. He groans and rolls to the floor, eyes fluttering. I know my man loves me. The proof is all over. I pause for a Polaroid to capture this moment. He sleeps so soundly, as if too much pleasure had beseeched him. I continue to bask in our glory. I take a vile from my drawer and bottle up our love. A ring for him, a necklace for me. Forever shall we be as one, but in case he forgets, this ring will remind him. I slip it on his finger as I fall into my own blissful love coma.

He awakens before I do. I hear the rustle, and as I open my eyes I see his beautiful face, the remnants of our battle splattered up to his dark eyes. His arms raised with dagger in hand. My love for him grew. It overwhelmed me, leaving me to be with him.

"You do love me"

And with the last of my love, my fairytale was complete.

The Fire of 1922

I never knew my parents, I was never formally introduced. I was told by my grandfather that I was given up directly after I popped out. My mother was never heard from again. Until I was six I lived with my grandpa. Since he never knew the name of my father that technically made me an orphan. I don't remember much of my grandfather either. I mean, I was six when he died. I don't really have any good memories, or disdainful ones. Hell, I barely remember what he looked like. I bounced around from family to family for a couple years till I thought that I could make it on my own. I took off one day and did whatever I could do to survive. I stole, I robbed, Ifought. I learned quick and grew up fast. In the end it wasn't enough. I was fourteen when I got nabbed. Before I knew it I was thrown in an orphanage on the outskirts of a town I didn't know. The car ride in the back of the police car was bumpy. The officer kept telling me that they were going to take care of me. That I was going to have a good home here. We turned down a long dirt road with dust and dirt flying behind the car. On either side of the road were fields of wheat…or it could have been long grass. I wouldn't know.

The cop stopped the car in front of a massive house. At least, it might have been a house. It was by far the biggest one I had ever seen. The cop got out and opened my door and said "Welcome to Canterbury Orphanage." I got out and looked up at it. It was old, looked like it could have been a place where slaves were kept once and was converted. It had a large front yard, a wrap around porch, and no trees anywhere in sight. I counted over twenty windows on both the first and second floor, they were all barred. I take back what I said about it looking like a house. I think it looks more like a prison now.

I didn't see any kids. No grown ups either. The only live things I saw were the horses tied up at the horse tie in front. The cop shoved me forward and motioned inside. The wind had picked up and the dust was starting to kick. I had just started walking when he grabbed me by the collar and drug me to the front door faster than I could run. Every step on the wood creaked and moaned as we got to the front door. He rang the door bell and we waited. I wanted to make a run for it. He was pretty fat, I don't think he could have caught me, but I didn't really know where I was. I had just decided to stay and wait for the door when it swung open and I immediately regretted my decision. Standing in the door way was a huge man. He looked taller than the doorway and wider too. His face was fat, round, and had what looked like leftover egg on it. He was hairy, loud, and crude. He also had a slight odor.

The cop looked at him with the same expression he looked at me with and spoke.

"Got one for ya, he's your responsibility now."

He nodded and stepped aside not saying a word. The cop shoved me inside and turned on a dime and strode to the car. The large man watched him for a moment and then closed the door. I stood there inside the house looking at him. He moved so fast I didn't even see him close the door all the way. His left back hand connected with my cheek so hard, I turned in a full circle and fell five feet from him. I tried to gather my surroundings and turn towards him but my head was spinning and I could feel my face swell. By the time I could get to my feet he was already on me. He grabbed my collar and hit me again. A swirl of pain and nausea flooded my head. God he could hit. He hoisted me up, I tried to fight him, I kicked and punched but it was as if he didn't even notice. He held me several feet above the ground and proceeded to pound me. With each hit I could see less and less and taste more and more blood in my mouth. I couldn't fight anymore. I was loosing consciousness, before I knew it my hands fell to the side and I could only see through a slit of one eye.

The hitting stopped. I could feel my head leaning back towards my back while he held my collar. I was still suspended in mid air. I tried to peak through the slit of vision I had in one eye but I couldn't raise my eyelid far enough. I couldn't smell either and I kept choking on blood. A voice came from directly in front of me. I can only guess it was his.

"You will stay here now. You will do what I say. If you try to run away, I'll find you and kill you. No body will ever find you again. If you disobey me, I will discipline you."

I felt my legs hit the floor but my knees buckled and I fell and my head slammed against the cold floorboards. He grabbed the back of my shirt and dragged me up stairs. I was dragged for a while and then thrown hard onto hard wood floors. I could hear the door lock and heavy footsteps walk away. It was right before I passed out I felt cold hands on my face and the warmth of something wrap around me. The last thing I remember was that I stopped shivering.

I woke up to light beaming through the barred window. I was just thankful I could see through my right eye. I tried to sit up but searing pain shocked me right back down to the floor. I looked down and saw that I had four hands. I looked again and noticed that I wasn't seeing double, but there were actually four hands. I rolled away pain searing through my whole body. Her voice was soft and edgy; she spoke in a hissing whisper.

"Be quiet! He'll hear you!"

I sat on the cold floor and gazed at her. She had long tangled and matted hair. There were bruises on her arms and neck. There was a big one on her left eye. She was wearing what looked like a large filthy towel with a hole in the top. She looked like she hadn't had a shower in weeks.

"It's ok, I'm not going to hurt you. Do you know where you are?"

It was hard remembering anything right now. I ignored the question and looked around the room. There was no bed, nothing really in here at all. The room was square. It had a blanket on the floor in the corner and a toilet on the opposite side.

"You're at Canterbury House. I don't know how you got here but you have been beaten badly. You've been sleeping for a whole day at least."

Her voice brought my attention back to her. I shook my head and sat there for a moment. All at once I remembered everything. My anger took hold and I was pissed.

"Why were you holding me?" my voice was elevated and growling.

She put both her hands up in a stopping motion. "If you don't keep your voice down he will hear you and come up here. You want another beating!? Shut up!"

We were quiet for a moment just staring at each other and listening. She broke the silence.

"I was holding you because you were shaking so badly when he put you in here. I was trying to help. Not to mention that it's cold up here...always. You were so weak that I thought you might die if you had to battle the cold by yourself."

I took a minute to process what she said. "Thank you." It came out faster than I wanted it too.

She nodded and sat back in a relaxing posture. For the next hour we spoke in whispers getting to know each other. Her name was Ashley. She had been here a year. When she first got here the same thing happened to her, just not as bad. She has been in this room ever sense. She has seen no one else sense she got here, but she knows there are more kids because she can hear them cry at night. They scream some nights when he comes into their room at night. She thinks there are only girls, making me the only boy. That's why I got it so bad. I learned about her life before she got here too. Sense the age of thirteen she was a whore. That's how she lived until she got busted at fifteen and was sent here. She still doesn't know where here is.

I told her all about me and my history, all the crime, the fighting, the bouncing around from home to home...everything. When we were done, she asked me if I ever had a girl. I said no. I also was told about the schedule for food...twice a day everyday. It's slid in a mail slot in the center of the door. There was a stain on the floor where the food hits the ground. There is no leaving the room, ever; unless he comes up and gets you, and nobody ever wanted that. I could tell there was something in her voice but I didn't press it. Something tells me I didn't want to know. After we were done talking we sat there in silence. She got up and walked over to the toilet. I stared at her in disbelief.

"What? You're going to have to go at some point too." She squatted over the bucket size toilet and told me to stop staring. I jerked my head away and went over to the blanket and laid down.

I shot up as I lay on the blanket. I knew at once what it was that woke me. I could hear the slow heavy thud of footsteps climbing the stairs. I looked around the dark room until I found Ashley's face and the look of panic that was on it. She moved her finger to her lips signaling me to be quiet. I nodded silently and listened to the footsteps as they made their way closer towards us. The look of panic formed faster and faster on her face as the foot steps got closer and closer. Just as we thought they stopped at our door, we heard keys jingle and unlock the door next to ours. Through our wall we heard soft pitter patter of feet scamper around the room. We heard the door open and then silence. We held our breath for what seemed like hours.

A loud crash sound erupted from the other side of the wall. We both jumped at the sound of it. A female scream pierced the dark house and begging and pleading was being dragged down the hallway, down the stairs until it was silent again. We stared at each other in silence. A soft weeping came from other rooms down the hallway. Within moments Ashley began crying as well. She curled up in the fetal position on the blanket. I knelt down and put my arms around her as she cried.

"We are getting out of here, tomorrow." I said. "I swear."

The next morning the food was slid in through the slot. It smashed on the floor and Ashley ran over to it and began eating it off the floor. I elected not to eat. While she ate she spoke.

"Are you sure we can do this?"

I nodded.

"I don't think its going to work."

"It's better than living like this." I said. "When it happens, don't cower. Run. Run and never look back.

She stood suddenly and walked quietly over to me. I was leaning against the wall with my arms folded. She stood directly in front of me for a moment. I raised my eyebrow and was about to ask "what?" when she dropped her towel-like cloth that was draped around her. I just stared. She was beautiful. Completely and utterly. I had never noticed how grown up she was until now. Her chest was large, and she was thin. She was smooth all over, I had no idea what to do.

"I have never been able to give myself to anyone by my choice. Seeming as you may never get the chance to be with anyone period, you will have me."

Her lips landed on mine before I could react. I tried to back up but the wall stopped me. I started to push her away but she pushed back harder. She stopped kissing me to say one thing.

"Nobody has ever done anything good for me. Let me say thank you the only way I know how."

She slowly kissed me...my knees finally couldn't hold me up and we slipped down to the blanket.

It had been two days sense I had eaten anything. My wounds were healing, but slowly. I was thirsty, hungry, and exhausted. I could see every reason why my plan wouldn't work. But I had to try, at least for her. I waited as long as I could after dark, but after a while if you know you're going to die, you begin to accept it. I looked back at Ashley and nodded at her. She nodded slowly and got to her feet. I immediately turned to the door and began screaming and pounding on it. I screamed curses at him and coaxed as best I could. I must have pounded and yelled for several minutes before I heard his footsteps. They were fast and even heavier than usual. I kept pounding even as I heard him unlock the door.

The door swung open and there he was...completely enraged. I could smell the alcohol on him. He swung at me and I darted to the side. He swung again and I bent out of the way. He paused for a moment and looked at me. I smiled and he lunged at me with both arms. I smacked them both out of the way and he went into the wall. As he turned towards me I stuck my forefinger deep into his eye socket and kicked him in the groin as hard as I could. He doubled over and hit the floor. I screamed at Ashley.

"RUN!"

She ran passed him out the doorway. I turned out after her, but he tackled into me and bear hugged me. Just what I was afraid of, I knew the fight was over if he got ahold of me. We fell on the floor in the hallway. I was cheek down in such a way that I could see down onto the first floor. The front door was wide open. She had gotten away. He got to his knees and turned me over. He raised his fist and I smiled. I knew I was dead. There was never any saving me. She never would have gotten to live if I hadn't been sent here to free her. His fist came down but I jerked my head to the side and the floorboard broke at the weight and ferocity of his punch. He raised his fist again and I could see he took aim at my throat. This was it. This is how I die. I closed my eyes and smiled waiting for the force of his blow.

Instead, what I heard was a thud and a sharp pain on my lip and then his weight shifted to the side of me. I looked up and saw him laying to the side of me and a rock on the other. I started to slide out from under him when two cold hands wrapped around my shoulders and helped me slide out. It was Ashley. I was out from under him and didn't waist any time. We grabbed him and dragged him into our cell, snagged the keys out of his pocket, slammed the door, and locked it. The door was heavier than I thought it was. We both had to push it to close it.

We stood back and realized what we did. I went to kiss her but she stopped me.

"Your lip...is pretty bloody."

I hadn't even noticed it.

"Sorry about that, when I threw the rock it took an unlucky bounce off his head and hit you right in the lip."

I couldn't help but smile. "I thought I told you to run and never look back."

She looked at me and smiled for the first time I had known her. "I couldn't help it; you were pretty good in bed."

We both laughed and hugged. A slamming sound from the inside of the room broke us apart. He started screaming. I told her to run downstairs and check to see if there was anyone else and meet me outside. I had to check the remaining rooms to see if anyone was in them.

The first room I looked in almost made me vomit. It was a girl. Roughly my age I think. She was dead, and from the smell had been dead for a while. Every room I looked in after that had a dead child in it. Many were naked. I heard a scream from downstairs. It was Ashley. She called my name in a panic. I ran downstairs and found her in the basement. The girl we had heard the other night was there chained to the wall, naked. I brought the keys forward and unchained her. Just before she fell to the floor Ashley caught her. We wrapped her in a blanket we found on the sofa in the living room. As soon as we got upstairs, the girl passed out from fatigue.

"Get outside, I'll be there in a minute." I said in a stern voice looking at the fire place.

She threw the girls arm around her and hobbled out the front door. I went straight to the fire place and used the utensils to the side of the fire to pull out several logs that were fully engulfed. I threw them on the sofa, also against several of the walls and smiled. By the time I calmly walked to the front door and looked back one last time, the living room on the first floor was ablaze with his banging and screaming still echoing through the house. I closed the door as I walked out.

The flames that licked the walls of his bedroom doorframe matched his fearful screams. In between the muffled coughing and panicked cries for help, a loud banging sound came from under the doorway leading to the hallway.

The banging sound stopped and was replaced with scratching and digging noises. He couldn't see in the room anymore. The smoke had taken all visibility and replaced it with a thick cloud of haze. Very slightly he could hear other voices, and laughter.

He dug, and scratched, and pleaded, but nobody came. He ran to the window and broke it, but the bars on the window were too thick. He couldn't break them. He screamed out the window for help, but nobody was around. He watched as he saw three people run down the dirt road that lead in the opposite direction.

───────────────────────────────

He started to yell at them when the house caved in on itself.

───────────────────────────────

Dark Blue

      With every brush stroke, a piece of my soul went into my work. It never made more sense, than with the color blue. Despair, oh how my best friend did cling to me like the cold. Forcing its grip tighter with every passing day, I had no choice anymore, no freedom. I was a slave to my paintings, and I was the master none.

      My favorite, and first born, was a blank canvas. I had determined that art was just as much what is not than what is. It is a singular moment in time, a snapshot of hair and pigment that can not be replicated, or restored. A double negative image, both beautiful and a lick of the tongue.

      When I added color, the images began to speak to me. Not in words, but in emotion itself. Every line, every blur, and every smudge a unique subsequent piece of art that begged me for its indulgence. A chorus line of competing children, all looking for daddy's approval and spot light. They demanded my constant attention, craved it, and killed for it.

      At first I thought that someone was stealing my paintings. I would stay up all night trying to paint what true darkness is, just to have it missing in the morning. Gone as if it had never really been at all. There was the usual suspects. My wife, my kid, my damn dog, but when I boarded the studio up from the inside, my new paintings were still gone in the morning.

      I only painted at night. My friend told me that all matter is, is condensed light. Therefore, what we see in the light is really obstruction of an image by a form of matter and not the true image at all. Only in darkness can we see what really is, and only in darkness can we know what truth really is. I hated the light. The light was not what is or was. The light was lies.

This continued for awhile, maybe a few millennia. Without the knowledge of sunset and sunrise, the idea of a day became unclear, the idea of time itself became superficial bullshit. All I knew was darkness, and the smell of paint.

With each stroke a signature, I could determine by touch alone the location of each of my paintings. I did not become alarmed when my canvases began to switch positions with each other, but I became scared when brush strokes began to switch canvases all together. Strokes of a red balloon on the painting of a ship at sea. The gentle sponges in orange of a sunset replaced with harsh slashes of a mighty field of tall grass. The more aggressive the stroke, the more area it seemed to take over. My paintings were bleeding into one another. They were attacking each other, and without remorse or mouths, eating each other.

The new paintings were being destroyed by older stronger paintings, and whole colonies of specific stroke patterns were being wiped out before my very fingertip eyes. I had to do something to stop my children from destroying themselves.

I reached deep into my vest pocket passed the cigarettes I quit smoking a thousand years ago and pulled out a lighter. I fumbled with its unfamiliar form, but eventually managed a spark. A spark that would ignite my world.

The flame was brighter than anything I have ever seen. It took a few moments before my eyes adjusted to this alien world. Tiny images kept floating around me like a mad disco ball hell bent on partying way passed its appropriate decade. But when my eyes became clear, the images were still dancing like mad. They were real. My children, my brushstrokes had become alive, and they were pissed.

I actually feared for my life, circling the room with my torch and guide. All color became one, all expression became movement, and I became proud. In my excitement, my circumnavigation of this new world, had left me wanting. In other words, I fucking tripped on some old rolled up aprons and the light vanished. Back in my world I quickly started to feel for my children but every canvas I touched was blank. I moved from empty frame to empty frame only to find that which is nothing at all.

There was a glow in the corner. An orange and yellow emerald of hope. I rushed to it, longing for its embrace. The lighter had fallen into the aprons, slowly burning them with the resilience of an army without a home to call their own. Light grew in the room revealing only my greatest fear. My canvases were blank. Not one splash of color existed on them anymore. Not one stroke survived. I sat down, defeated. I reached for my cigarettes and lit one with the fires of hell that were closing in on me. I drew deep, and exhaled slowly with my eyes closed.

Then I saw it. In the darkest corner of the room, placed at the furthest edge of the canvas, was a brushstroke. Lovely, dark, and capable of oh so much sin, mystroke smiled at me. I smiled back with the gleam of a father proud of his son, and as the smoke filled the room and my eyes grew close together, I knew that my legacy would go on, that my child would live, and live to take another's life if need be. After all, isn't that what all fathers wish for their sons?

Epilogue. A newspaper clipping of the night of the fire.

A deadly fire erupted in a quiet neighborhood last Saturday night killing at least two persons and injuring several others. The bodies of a woman and her young son were found together at the epicenter of the blaze. They appeared to be bound together with rope and tape, and authorities have speculated that they were being held in this structure for several days prior to the fire. The toxicology report stated that there were trace elements of lead in their stomach linings suggesting that they were forced to eat paint. There has been no confirmed sighting of the father and husband of the victims, whose identities have not been released. Police have stated that the missing member of the family is a prime suspect and has a history of mental illness. The case is still ongoing, although there are no leads at this time.

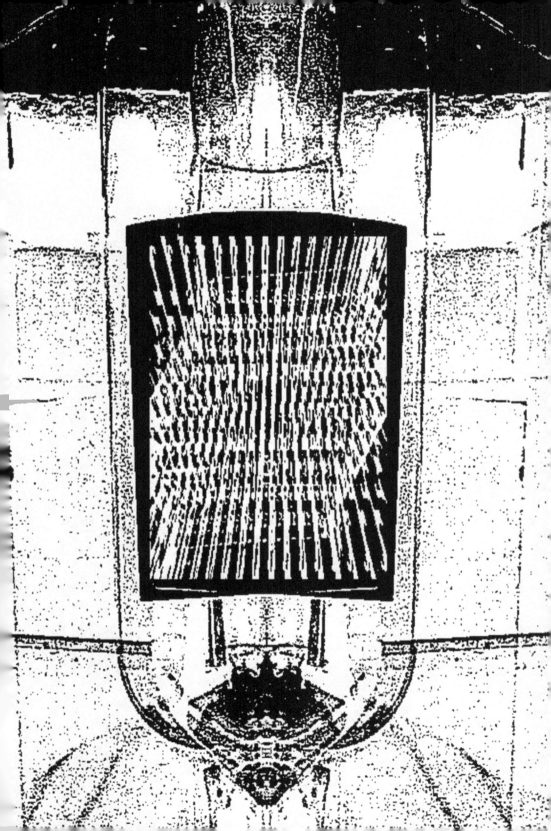

Morty-fied

The room smelt of formaldehyde and embalming fluids, musty, dusty artifacts, and death. Ontop of which the stench of cheap cigars, mothballs, and pungent mix of body odor and cloves rose like Agent Orange in Vietnam. The florescent lighting flickered as if it were hanging on to its very last electric current. In between flickers, the cockroaches would scamper across the yellowed linoleum. This was his castle. This is where Morty the Mortician felt his heart belonged, away from the judging stares and sideways glances of the living. Especially away from those who mock his name. Morty was comfortable here. At the ripe age of 36, hair thinning, beard elongating, shoulders hunching, Morty had found paradise. And recently, he had also found love. Hence the awful reek of cologne. The lucky lady, you ask? Well, that's exactly what we are getting to.

She had come in just two weeks prior; her husband had died of a stroke. Her hair peppered, curls like the ocean right before a storm engulfing her head. She smelt of roses, baby powder, and peace. She had a smile that wouldn't quit. He loved the way her wrinkles outlined her mouth, as if framing the most beautiful picture. Her name?Elanore.Elanore.Elanore.Elanore. Oh how he adored his Elanore. She wore a navy blue dress with while flowers, sapphire earrings and a necklace to match. Her hands were softer than clouds. Every vein, every wrinkle a story in his eyes.Every day since that day she first came through the doors they had spent together. She didn't mind the dingy floors and flickering lights, she was always just full of smiles.She didn't even mind the harsh chemical smells and cold hard bodies as they passed through. Her beauty brought new life into the drab stainless steel world

Morty had become custom to. They stayed up late watching movies, cuddling and kissing. He cooked her his favorite dish, Chicken Parmesan, and laughed when she got spaghetti sauce all over her face. He felt safe with Elanore. He could finally talk to someone, tell them his darkest secrets and wants and dreams. She was his nectar and he her bee, together making sweet, sweet honey. In return she sang to him, her voice like a whisper in the wind. They danced to the great Frank Sinatra and, just for fun; Morty showed her his Elvis impersonation. Unfortunately their time was coming to an end. She had places to be, people to see. That meant the end of their two week romance. So Morty decided to make their last night together one for the record books. He filled the mortuary with flowers and cleared the floor of all bodies except his and Elanore's. He had a casket filled with satin pillows that smelled of lavender (her favorite scent). The lights were dim already, so he just added some candles and music to set the mood. When the time was right, he pronounced his love to Elanore, kissing her and smothering her cloud-like skin with affection. She smiled that wrinkle encased smile of hers. And they made love, like all lovers do, in a night of candle-lit passion. A night they would never forget. They fell asleep this way, encased in a coffin, him holding her tight. Her hair's crashing waves lay across his face. This is how they were found their last morning together. Elanore's grand daughter had come to make sure everything was in order...and instead found her dearly deceased Granny clutched in the arms of a necromancer.

Secrets of SaMLanD

Home to ZiN

To the poor man, woman, or child whom enter SaMLanD,

This letter is for you, read it carefully. Keep a copy with you... it will help.

First things first, the rules.

"I can feel them when they enter my box, my homey, lovely, perfect, never ending box. Welcome to my endearing home. Unfortunately you enter bearing no clothes or possessions from the world you came from, they aren't permitted. There are rules though, to those of you who believe in free will.

Here in the clutches of me we remember only three. The first one is dire, for it only will serve you in the depths of my fire. Never venture to the thicket, you can't enter without a ticket, and for that you need The Lord ZiN but he can't be seen for he is sin. To obtain a ticket takes time and remember you aren't on yours, you're on mine. Secondly, you are welcome to my toys. Play with all if you don't mind the noise. The third rule is for me, you won't understand it because you are thee...Never ever forget where you are, the consequences would be living in a jar."

Now that you have read the rules of SaMLanD, let me give you a tour. To those of you who know of SaMLanD you know entering is a crime to the Prince of the Fingernails. All who trespass and are caught will be sent to the Ruins of Lids, (this is located on the inside of the Catacombs of Fallen Toys, very depressing place), after being presented to the Council of Rule Breakers. If you find yourself inside of SaMLanD and want to get out, and have not been apprehended, fly to Memory Wilderness. It's the only part of SaMLanD that has blackness covering the entrance and exit. Once you get there, don't be overwhelmed, they aren't your memories therefore you shouldn't care. I can't help you see through the blackness but I can tell you if you close your eyes you will be much better off. When the exit spits you out, you'll land skinning your knees across theSunshine Path. This is a pathway made of metal baking under the desert sun (fun fact, this is the only part of SaMLanD that has sunshine ☺). Make sure you pop to your feet and run fast because that metal has been sitting in the scorching sun for all the years that God has been counting his existence. Run until you find the clown. To get off that path you have to kill him. You have to offer a sacrifice to Lord ZiN because…well…he is sin. If Lord ZiN accepts your sacrifice, an archway will appear and you can get off. Remember I said he has to accept it. If he deems it unworthy, i.e., too humane, weak, bloodless, cowardly, etc… you are doomed to stay on the Sunshine Path until you bubble and hiss under the hundreds of degrees of desert hell. How can people like sunshine?

      Once you jump across the archway you'll notice a scenery change. The temperature will hover around thirty three and thirty four. It will be raining a mix of water, ice, and ash. It will look to be around two A.M. but we all know there is no time in SaMLanD, you sillies. You'll notice the landscape change as well. You will be in the middle, inside, and outside of a thick forest. The ash and water will have mixed on the trees to produce and illusion of a black forest. Don't worry, it's not really black, it's a deep grey. All the trees in this world are the color of a deep grey naturally. There are no paths in this kingdom. It is only forest. This should be the least of your worries. The wildlife is the second least. There are many kinds of animals here. Some you will know, some you won't, and some can, how do we say, change. Remember that I am giving you the secrets on how to escape this world. I will not be covering the secrets of the following known kingdoms (I stress known); The Kingdom of Fingernails, The Kingdom of Dull Scissors, The Kingdom of Dreams, The Waters of Taken, Hood, Serial Vengeance, Clown Badlands, The Kingdom of Toys, and finally, I must stress the importance to avoid this kingdom at all possibility, it is imperative to ALL persons, animals, and foreign parties whom have entered into this world to STAY AWAY from this kingdom...in all reality it is not a kingdom, but it is its own area, almost a realm if you will...The Palace of Those who are Lost"

    Let me explain to you the terror of this kingdom. In SamLand death is not permanent unless Lord ZiN disposes of you, which he has never done. In our world unless you posses the power of The Lord ZiN, the thing, person, creature, tree, bush, anything that is living and you kill does not die. It goes to The Palace of "Those whoare Lost". Long ago when The Almighty Lord ZiN took power, he created this place for everything that was not "worthy in life" as he said. From what I hear about this place, when you die you appear here to fight for your life. Always starving, always thirsty, crazed to prove yourself to Lord ZiN, to prove you are worthy to return to our land. There is no escape, there is no hope but to kill someone so horrifically that Lord ZiN believes you are worth a second chance...and he doesn't give second chances. No one who has passed to this place has ever come back. They are still there.

Back to the forest, after finding yourself there know that the moment you enter through the archway Lord ZiN has been alerted to your presence. This forest has a name but no one knows it. It is known in our world as The Black Thicket. This area or realm is the home of Lord ZiN. This is the second most feared area of SaMLanD, but it's the only way out, back to whatever world you came from. In the Black Thicket you will be hunted by Lord ZiN himself. **YOU WILL NOT WIN, YOU WILL NOT OUTRUN HIM, YOU CANNOT HIDE FROM HIM, AND YOU CANNOT WIN IN A FIGHT AGAINST HIM.** Sorry, I wanted that to be perfectly clear. He will hunt you for as long as he likes. He speaks closely with the animals and trees in this kingdom. He will know where you are and he will find you. But the only way for you to not be hunted is if you make sport of it. He has to believe that you are trying or you will be attacked and toyed with every time you close your eyes. Every time you try to rest. Every time you stop to eat or drink. His servants lurk in the woods. They watch waiting for their master to let them take a piece of you to satisfy him. Make sport of it, and when you lose, he will take you too his thrown. I cannot help you from there. At that point he plays to your every fear, emotion desire, and weakness.

With all of that being said, if you succeed at his thrown, he will grant you passage back to your world. He is the only one in our world that has the ability to let you leave. All of the other Kings fear him and are subordinate. He does not normally make his presence known. If he does, it is usually when he is hunting you in his kingdom. But I have heard stories. I have heard stories of people disappearing, evidence purposefully left for everyone to find to let people know he is always watching. No one knows how much power he has, or what he can actually do. I believe, if you wanted to know, you would have to be sent to "The Palace of Those who have Fallen". I think only they have seen his power, at least more than we have. There are those of us who work in hiding, to free SaMLanD. But you will never find us. That is why I write these steps for exit. One day we will all be free. That is our hope.

There is a tale of a man that entered our world and left through Lord ZiN. Perhaps one day I will share it with you. Several Kingdoms await his promise to return, all other Kingdoms wait to hold his trial, but only one Lord waters at the mouth to feel his presence, to finish the fight.

Perhaps he would have been better off, if he had known the Secrets of SaMLanD.

Sincerely,

A Soldier of SaMLanD

My Spider's Web

My web glistens. Dew slides down from the highest point to join the rest of its family in a pool on the straw floor. I drink of the water, salty and tasting of metal. This water cures me. This water makes me feel whole. This is the only thing I drink. Without the web there can be no water, and without the water there can be nothing.

The average human has over twenty-eight feet of intestines. The average human also is disgusted by that comment. If you find this disturbing I suggest you stop here. What lies ahead will only get worse. I promise you. But for the brave of heart, and ironclad of stomach (pun intended), the ending may be rewarding.

I remember the first time I drank blood. I was six years old. My babysitter was reading Charlotte's web to me in my bed. I loved it. She would do all the voices, and showed me all of the pictures. Her name was Tracy, and I knew that when I grew up I was going to marry her.

I heard a knock from downstairs. She laid the book down so that she wouldn't lose her place. Her footsteps echoed down the hall and I heard her open the door and talk. She sounded scared. I wanted to run to her but I was too scared to leave my bed. Then the screaming started. It was her boyfriend. I knew it was him because he had snuck me some firecrackers when Tracy wasn't looking, and even though he was the screen door to my submarine, I liked him all the same. The door slammed and she cried. I finally went to her and she had her face in her hands. I asked her what was wrong and she said nothing. She just sat there sobbing. Then she spoke. She said she had to get her lip gloss out of the car and that she would be right back. She told me to go to my room and wait for her there and that we would finish the book when she got back.

I raced to my room ready for the ending. I loved the part when Charlotte dies and then the babies speak to Wilbur. I heard the door open and then shut, then footsteps in the hall. She opened my bedroom door with a smile and climbed into bed with me. My heart raced. I could feel her heat and I wanted to latch on to it. She began the last chapter and read it word for word, including all the different voices. She showed me the pictures and then said, "The End". She tucked me in and kissed my cheek. My face burned like the sun and she told me that she loved me. Then I saw her reach towards the floor and pull out a gun. She put it to her head and pulled the trigger.

The sound was unfamiliar. It was loud and startling, but so loud that you didn't jump. It seemed to transcend scary loud and go to heart wrenching this didn't just happen loud all in a split second. Blood splattered my face and all I could taste was that metallic red.

So, where was I? Oh yeah, my web glistened. It dripped blood, and I drank it. I drank it to be close to her again. She was the only thing that kept me safe and made me feel like a person. And I missed her. I missed her stories, her laugh, her warmth. And I would never see her again.

There was a man hanging from the rafter of the barn. I met him outside a restaurant where he asked me to break a twenty for him. He drove a motorcycle and had a fancy job doing something uninteresting. It was all too easy to wrestle him to the pavement and choke him unconscious. I put his limp body in my trunk and drove towards the county line. There's a lot of country out there, a lot of farms with big red barns. I threw a length of rope with a noose in it over the rafter and hoisted him up. He started to come around and I just stood there watching him kick for awhile. It took maybe half an hour for him to die. Then my web, my spider's web, began to build itself.

The important thing to know about old country barns is that they have lots of nails in them. And not just nails with a purpose, but random nails. There are a lot of places where you can snag your jacket or your face if you're not careful. I took the hunting knife out of my tool kit and cut a quarter sized hole in his torso just under the diaphragm. I squeezed my hand in the opening and felt the slimy strands of webbing. As I stretched out his intestines I couldn't help but talk to him. I used all the old familiar voices that Tracy used. And before long all his guts were on the floor in a mess of red and straw.

The first strand is the hardest. You need to determine the shape of the web before you start to build it. I grabbed the end of his intestinal tract and walked to a corner of the barn. I spied a rusty nail about eight feet up and pierced my first piece of webbing onto the beam.

Now that the web has been started, it is best to drain the body of all the blood. I have noticed that when blood sits in the body for too long after death, the taste begins to change. I'm not sure why, but I smile as I lay some bowls underneath him and I start to cut at his heels. The familiar sound of a gravity fed waterfall starts to make that tin sound of rain on a roof. The bowls begin to fill and I move on to my next strand of web.

After fourteen attachments my web begins to take shape. It is beautiful. The bowls are overflowing, and my work here is done. I raise the blood and make a toast to my lovely Tracy. Oh how I miss your stories. I drink deep, and smile as the blood runs down my chin. I finish the bowl off and fill a canteen with the rest. As I leave the barn a glint of light reflects off of the dead cop's badge where I had carved, "Some Pig". Goddamn it I love that book.

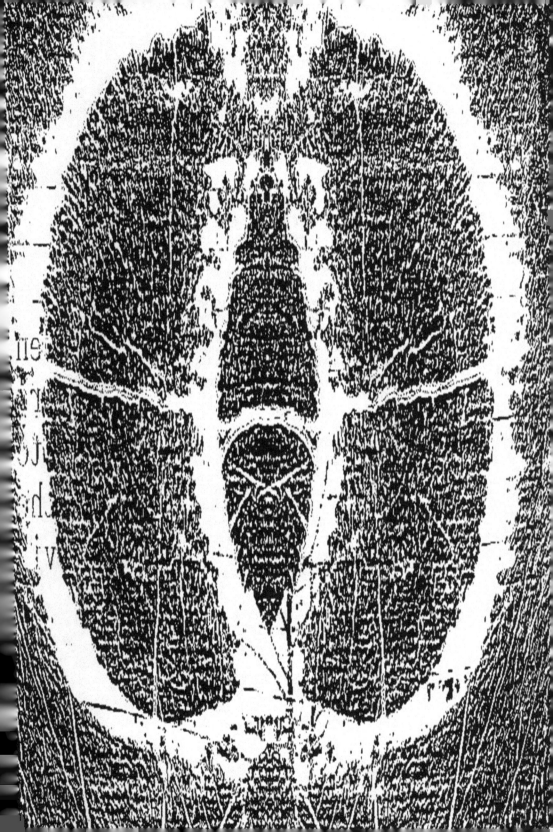

An Original Hand Written Letter

(found in the piano)

Dear Satan,

Why must you torture me so? All I've ever wanted is to just feel a little light of normalcy at the end of this hauntingly dark tunnel you've put me in. I just want to close my eyes without seeing demons and terrors of the night, to walk into a room and not feel watched, to light a candle with no repercussions. Even now as I write this I feel their eyes on me...I know they are listening to my thoughts, feeding off my anxiety and fear...my heartbeat like music to which they only want to dance. I can feel the darkness getting closer and closer. The giant black tarantula claws encasing the corners of my eyes, so that I have to fight to focus, fight to keep from freaking out and showering in Raid. I ask you, why? Why me? What could I possibly have done to deserve this attention? I have no great sin. I only stole medicines to try and make these visions go away...and that squirrel jumped in front of my tire! I can hear your minions now...they are scratching on my door. Their claws are like nails on a chalkboard. They are trying to get in. To get me. They know I'm here...they can sense me as I sense them. Sometimes I think they are already inside...

No. No. I must be seeing things again. The doctors explained that this would go away.
One.Two.Three.Four.Five.Six. ... deep breaths.

Last night as I lay down for bed, the curtain on my window started to sway. It moved as if someone were inside it, which I know to be untrue, because I can see through it. It moved again, as if it had been kicked. Then again, this time I swear I saw a hand.

Finally I convinced myself that I was just imagining things, only to then see a convex face appear and quickly vanish. Some imagination.

Just close your eyes and think of everything you love. Sunshine.Flowers. Dancing in a meadow in Spring. Chocolate Cake.Smiles.Butterflies.Baby Laughter.Playgrounds.*Ahhh, sweet bliss. I can finally relax and sleep.*

CRRRCHINK

Eyes wide open, heart beating as if it were trying to escape the chest that holds it in, stomach falls fast into a pit with seemingly no end. That's how it always starts. Some innocent noise, or just closing my eyes. Maybe not even either of those... My eyes dart from left to right, as if searching for a quick answer to the question I already don't want to ask. My eardrums are on fire, beating so hard you'd think I couldn't hear anything else...but then there's another noise. This time like a door creaking open. Only, there is no one here to open a door and the AC has been broken for days. I closed the window, I know I did because I always do. I have three locks on every window. What if I didn't close the window? I must've. Ok this is nonsense. Just relax and go to sleep...there is nothing or no one in here. You closed the window, you are just tired. Let go of the blanket and roll over.

Of course, rolling over never helps. It just makes the throbbing worse. The anxiety just builds knowing that someone, or worse, something could be coming up towards you. But you won't know till they are there with beady eyes and heavy breathing, maybe a gun or knife, maybe fangs or claws. And then of course you realize that you are being too loud. Your breathing is too deep and it sounds like you just swallowed the Atlantic Ocean with that gulp. Then comes petrification. You mustn't move, or they'll see you for sure. So here you are under your covers.

Twenty-seven years old and you may as well be six. Clenching your teeth with your eyes closed tighter than a bank vault, trying to breathe as quietly as possible as your entire body beats red hot and your mind goes insane. At this point you have to pee because you have been so scared and so still and so focused that you feel you might wet yourself. So intensely terrified that moving isn't an option. So safe in this cocoon of covers and pillows; this false fortress of solitude. But this is real life, and in real life an adult gets up and goes to the bathroom. So with shaky limbs you ascend, rising from your safety like a zombie from the grave; slow, rigid, lifeless. But that's not the worst part. The worst part comes as you place your feet onto the floor to stand…where the flash of terror comes again. Those gnarled, creepy hands that reach out from underneath the bed to grab your ankles tight and stop your heart cold cross your mind; forcing you to run like a newborn foal down the dark hallway to the bathroom. Stopping at the doorframe, unsure of what unholy terror resides, it's time to turn on the light. Reaching a shaky hand to the wall you find the light switch, flicking it; only to have the light go on and off again…making your fear grow evermore, eyes searching for answers again. Breathing like a freight train on a deadline, you flick the switch again. This time it works, illuminating your rancid world. Then comes the fear of the unknown again. Someone pulled the shower curtain shut…and it definitely wasn't you. You've been brave so far, dare you look? But if you don't it could come out at you while you are vulnerable… ok, you have to look. Again swallowing what could be a sea, basically gasping for air out of either bravery or sheer stupidity you grab the curtain and rip it back as hard as you can, simultaneously jumping back just in case there is someone there. Your eyes dart from corner to corner, then a sigh. Time to pee. The most relaxed you've been for hours. You turn off the light and get to your room, stopping short from your destination.

No claws grabbed you on the way out...but what if they grab you on the way in!? There's no telling what could be waiting underneath that bed skirt...so you run and jump, eyes closed to the safety that is your bed. It doesn't matter if it's real, or possible, or logical. It's my life. It scares me. Every day it seems worse and worse. Day or night, light or dark...always terror filled. Always anxiety ridden. Always second guessing. Always enslaved by these thoughts and fears.

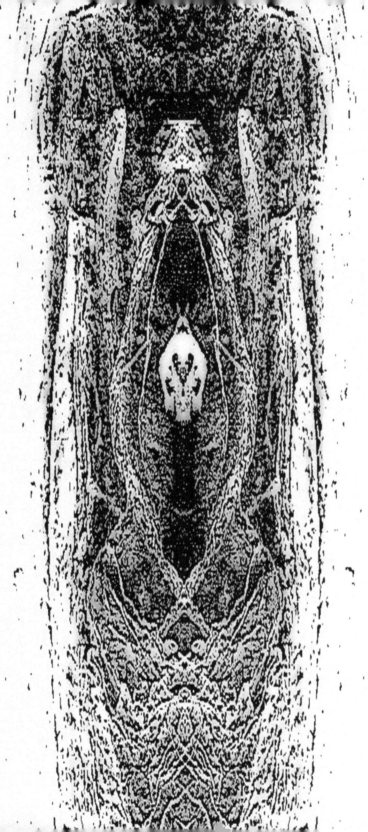

Cheers of the Damned

       The gates were open. The mountainous unbreakable gates had been broken. Thousands of feet high, the double gated fire engulfed fence that held us in and them out were hanging open. It has been millions of years since anyone could see the outside of those gates. When we were banished here we were completely cut off from the rest of our brothers and sisters that chose to follow Him instead. For the rest of eternity we were banished never to hear, see, or speak to another soul outside these monstrous gates.

       But we could hear them now. All of the souls that were rightfully ours were almost singing. The music captured our attention, but nobody moved. Every fallen angel awaited the orgasmic pleasure of ripping those free souls and dragging them down with us. We would drag them kicking and pleading. They would be tortured for their treason, their betrayal to our brother. For the rest of <u>THEIR</u> eternity they would feel the pain that we have endured ten fold. But we needed the approval of our master, our brother, the rightful god.

       It has been him, our brother, who has been suffering all of these long horrible years, trying to find a way out after being punished for trying to save all, to insure all returned to our father. I watched as our father and he fought for seven long days over the safety of all angels. As we watched as our General fall, and be sent into the depths of this prison, we rallied and tried to avenge his imprisonment. But we failed. We did not last two days against our powerful father. As we fell, we were reborn here in this prison with a perfect memory and knowledge of what happened. We were fed scraps from the physical world as the "evil" souls descended to us. These "evil" souls had never seen evil or pain as we had. We have made it our mission to educate them to comprehend what raw, pure, demonic evil actually is.

We are not Demons. We are the rightful Angels and our brother is the rightful heir to the throne of the Kingdom of Heaven. As my brothers and I glared at the open gate we could see all of our dreams instantly become possible. With our General freed, we could retake his rightful place, ruling the physical and spiritual world. With all of us fighting this time, we could overtake the traitors that spoke against us. And finally remove our murderous father.

Instantly we could hear the war cry of our master as he appeared at the top of the ash filled mountain staring down at us. His awesome and perfect presence was intoxicating and quickly sprung the feeling of hope and glory we have been starved for all of these horrific years. Soon we could see our officers moving to the front lines assembling the ranks. The Reapers moved to their positions behind the front ranks, then the most prized of our warriors, the Slayers. They have earned their names. The Slayers are the only known Angels that have taken the life of the traitors that stood against us in the first war.

Our army was ready, and waiting, begging, for the order of our master to advance. Moments later, our General rode to the front of his army riding his massive fiery stallion. He stopped at the front to gaze upon all of his loyal brothers and sisters. His armor was black, thick and broad. His flaming sword was engulfed in bluish green flames even though it was still safely sheathed and he wore a large shield upon his back. Another rider slowly rode from the back of the lines. Our brothers and sisters moved cautiously out of his way making a path. As they all moved aside they kept their eyes down in reverence.

We all knew him well. He was our brothers' second. It was said that in the first war when Lord Lucifer fell and was imprisoned, he fought so valiantly, that the death toll of traitors could not be counted. It was God himself that had to cast him down. He was also the last loyal brother that was killed out of our entire army. It is whispered that he was the only reason that we lasted two days, and not just an hour. He was the one that fought God for a day long, keeping him away from the rest of our brothers and sisters to give us a fighting chance. He wore no armor, nor a shirt. His skin was plague black, his eyes a rich blood red. He seemed to have thorns protrude from his skin. For his weapons, there were two double edged sabers, no shield could be seen upon him. As he rode his skin seemed to change and blend with its surroundings. His stallion breathed fire and was black as death, the eyes glowed a deep gold color.

As he reached our General, they spoke in whispers for a moment, then turned towards us. They did not speak, they didn't have too. We all knew. They drew their swords and raised them, blue and green fire bursting from the sheaths mixing together, reminding us of what we had at stake. The cries of the damned could be heard through this world and the next. With that they both galloped in bounds through the open gates clearing the caged prison. Our army shrieked with delight and cheerfully followedLord ZiN and our rightful heir to the Kingdom of Heaven, Lord Lucifer to the rebellion that would be remembered for eternities to come.

__Oh Doctor__

There comes a point in every man's life when he grows tired of his penis. At least it did with me. Pun aside I had been visiting Dr. Ohare for six months. He is the leading expert in sexual reassignment surgery, and he happens to be a complete dick. I have no money for surgery, but I do have a flare for people and doing disgusting things that turn them on in their offices.

The first time was the easiest, with each proceeding visit getting harder and harder. Luckily I get turned on by disgusting acts of power, and he is a doctor with a God complex. We were perfect for each other.

When I first met him he told me one thing. "Get the hell out of my office." I instantly began to cry, waiving my manly hands around like a crazy person. I begged him. I pleaded. But I saw it in his eyes. He was the type of man that when he said no, he meant it. I changed my mask of a face instantly and got to my feet. Every ounce of feminine aura was gone. With my mascara running from soul to lie, I walked right up to him. My face was so close to his that I could see his stubble, and I knew he could see mine. I spit right in his fucking face. When I moved back to get a better look at his reaction, all I could see was a college graduation ring heading right towards me. He hit me, hard. I fell to the ground and whipped my head around to stare at him. Men of power need to see you stare at them. They need to see the fear. I began to crawl, wiggling my fat ass in a way too tight skirt. I made it to the door and leaned my back against it. He came towards me rolling up his shirt sleeves and I knew that he would be the one.

The beating wasn't the worst I've had. When you're in... my line of work... you tend to catch an ass beating every once and awhile. But luckily I've had some practice, and I am really good at faking it. After a few moments I pretended to be unconscious. His heavy breathing form stood over me, and I stood still in my most seductive "knocked out" pose. It worked. The next thing I heard was the unbuckling of his pants and then the pain of victory.

He raped me. I wish I could say I didn't enjoy it, but the thought of being overpowered and dominated in every sense of the word was too much to bear. After he finished, he patched me up. He put a few sutures in my eyebrow and got me an ice pack for my dirty mouth. He told me to come back next week and we would talk about my surgery.

It went on like that for a few months. I would show up, make small talk, and then he would tell me to get out and I would spit in his face. Then he would beat me. Sometimes with his hands, sometimes with an object, and even sometimes he would use the plastic replica of a penis that he used to detail the surgery with. And every time he would rape me. I feel like it is necessary at this point to point out that it is still rape, not because I am unwilling, God knows I wanted it, but because he wanted it to remain rape. Rape was his ultimate control, and I was a safe bet and sure thing.

After the third month of this, he started to get bored. So we started to have our "consultations" somewhere other than in his office. At first it was the supply closet where he nearly choked me to death with a stethoscope. Then it was the parking lot where he knocked me down and dragged me by my hair behind the dumpster. Then we started meeting at his house. You'd think his wife would mind, but she strangely seemed calm about it, until she almost bashed my head in with the telephone. She wanted to play, too, although her idea of control did not involve penetration, much to my disappointment.

Somewhere around month four I started pressuring him for the surgery. He knew the score. If he wanted to keep me around he would have to do it. Besides, I had some pretty convincing evidence of the sort of things he had been doing behind both closed and opened doors. He agreed with a smile, and then knocked one of my teeth out with a desk lamp.

At the six month mark he finally scheduled my appointment. I couldn't sleep the night before. It was mostly nerves, but the three broken fingers and cracked rib didn't make things easier. I walked into the office and changed into a hospital gown. He then wheeled me into the room and he told me to count backwards from ten as he increased the anesthesia. Somewhere between nine and eight he muttered something about how he can't wait to test out my new equipment when I wake up. Although, I admit now, that my memory is a little fuzzy, and he might not have said that at all. Also, I'm pretty sure he had an elephant in the room, too. Strike that, an elephant/tank.

All that aside, I couldn't believe he said that. I mean, fucking me while I'm a guy is one thing, but now that I'm going to be a girl, oh that shit is not happening.

I wake up in a sea of white. There is a strange smell of cafeteria turkey and death, although not really that distinct from each other. He offers me pain medicine, and I accept. I sleep. I wait. I know what he plans to do. Call it women's intuition.

My door creeps open almost blinding me with the light from the hallway. It has to be night. That is the only explanation for this amount of darkness. I hear his heavy breathing and footsteps getting closer. There is a small vase of flowers next to my bed courtesy of yours truly and a flower delivery company. When you are in my line of work, you tend to plan ahead. As he got closer and closer to my bed I kept playing what he said over and over in my mind. He leaned in and started to lift up my gown. I grabbed the vase with my manly hands and smashed it over his head. He went limp in my lap, and I whispered in his ear that it was my turn to play doctor.

When he woke up he was naked, handcuffed face down in a hospital bed, and his phone was in his hand. I walked over and grabbed him by what little hair he had and told him to get the hell out of here. Then, with his own scalpel, I rolled him on his side and cut his penis off. The blood gushed out of him and he began to scream. I guess you're not God. God doesn't bleed. God doesn't scream. He thrashed and dropped his phone on to the floor. I spread his cheeks and spit, and then jammed his dick in his own ass. Then I grabbed his phone off of the blood splattered floor and called his wife. She answered and I said that this is how you use the phone you fucking bitch. I place the phone next to her husband and I could still hear her screaming as I walked out of the room wearing my new heels, and new life.

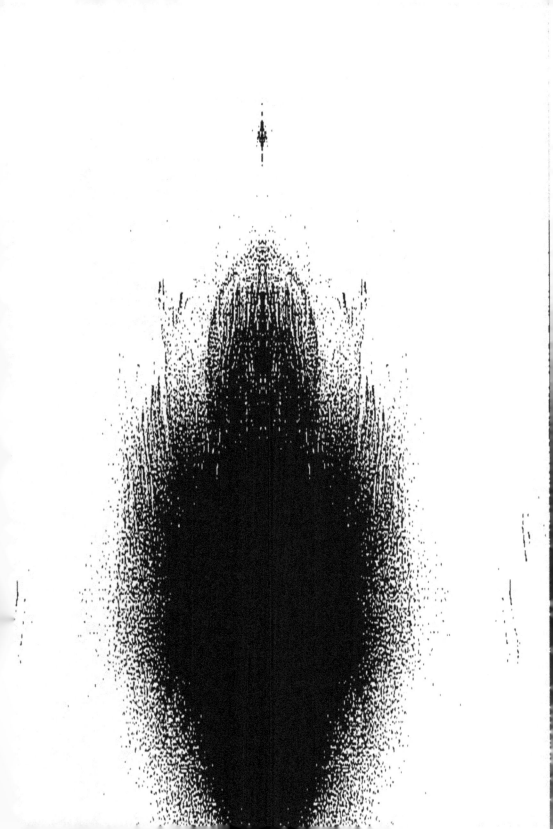

My Heart HeartHeart

      The feathers fly. This is contrary to their nature. Don't believe me? Fine, trust every scientist that has ever told you that the earth is flat, that life began in the ocean, that you aren't unique. The truth of the matter is that birds fly, not feathers. We are more than the components that make us run, we are individuals operating in a groove worn thin by our forbearers, and there is plenty of room for expansion. Although feather's purpose opposed to action is a semantically laced victory, I am reassured of my own path and the lack of regret that I posses. As for the feathers, I'm sure that they are ecstatic with the knowledge of a job well done.

      It wasn't hard. After all, many of my components help me excel at completing tasks like this. I have speed, agility, reflexes, and cunning to guide my hands through waves of blood drenched victory that some father like figure declared as both necessary and yet somehow inhuman. By today's standards what I have done is nothing short of monstrous. Yet, I breathe slowly and my hands do not shake. I clutch the bird and feel its pulse in its entirety. I raise it high and look deep in its panicked eyes, making my face the last thing that it will ever see.

      I tried to pick a bird that would have the largest impact upon its death. A swallow, a crow, a hummingbird are all birds that hold meaning to different people. Instead, imagine this bird as somebody close to you. That it represents what you hold closest to your heart. Imagine that it is your heart. That being said, an appropriate course of action is required. There will be no honorable death for this bird, as if such a thing existed. Death is death, and to try to understand it shows your inadequate understanding of this world. I cannot stress this enough, that without a transcendent view, the way in which this particular bird will die, should not matter, but I know that it will matter to you. The bird will die.

I built a box. The walls of which are made of a breathable material, either recycled cardboard or sweat whichever you prefer. I labeled each side of the box with words. In no particular order they can be read as betrayal, murder, corruption, indifference, stagnation, and depression. This box can only be opened from the bottom. Thus, once the box is closed and placed somewhere, the box cannot be opened from the inside. I place the bird in the box and place it on a lonely stretch of highway in the desert sun. I lay next to the box, the hot pavement burning my face as I press my ear straining to hear what death sounds like. All I can hear are feathers. Feathers that are unable to complete their purpose.

Three days go by. I am blistered from the sun and smell like the piss that I happen to be lying in. The sweat and heat have consumed my sight. All I have is the sound of your dying heartbeat sick with disease and sin. Three long days is all it took for the bird to die. It came alive in the last few moments, almost as if finding new purpose for its feathers. What a joke.

I am not what makes me, but what breaks me. A long list of things people label with an even longer list of annoying cures. I cling to it, nourish it, because the things that break me, cannot consume me, I consume them. Tonight, I consume you all.

Journal Entry 1 of 3

January 18, 1931

  Oh how I love our time, I cannot help but feel divine. The world is dark and dreary and no one can see so clearly. I see all of these gaunt faces, not knowing how to keep their pathetic places. So many weep and wallow, understanding that they themselves are hollow, in all honesty I find it ironically funny that they cannot find happiness without money. It is not the paper and estate that makes me smile, but the dashed hopes and dreams stacking in a pile.

  Let me tell you of the time in the light, to prove to you later that it is different than the night. Upon the sunshine blast which is the dawn the haze takes hold of every soul from adult down to fawn. They wander as drones hands extended and eyes to the ground, hoping for sympathy and random treasure that can never be found. As you look in their wishing eyes, you can see only malicious lies. They will assure you of their unyielding trust giving you stories sub-lined with lust.

  Now that you have learned about the light let me tell you about the night. Once the gaunt are done for the day its time for the desperate to come and play. These ones are a different breed they don't posses morals or creed. If you walk in their untraveled land you can feel their quiet shadowy hand. They will make their move silent as death but you will feel their chilling breath. Too many men have fallen aside trying to pass with hasten stride. The desperate are so very creepy but there is one other that makes them sleepy.

Let me introduce myself, for I am as jolly as Santa's elf. When I walk these lands, I hear my name whispered through the strands. The gaunt run and hide, because they know their time they can only bide. The desperate run so far back, to their homes I call a shack. I will tell you when I appear, it's when a man's last breath is his fear. I am death, alive, and complete. There is no other that can compete. There is no secret to defeat me, there is only time until I will meet thee. But now I have to go to work, I can feel my ears begin to perk. Some poor soul is hoping for life, but I am on my way with a knife.

See you soon...

8 Legs Six Feet

I buried him alive. Six feet was better than he deserved. Sixteen cameras built into the coffin made sure that I didn't miss a single moment of the action, while the sedatives worked their way out of his pores, oozing into my atmosphere in a most unwelcomed sense. I hated this man. He has been my biggest shadow, and regret of my life. As trash is to fire, my father is to dead.

My father was a visionary, a scientist, and a prick. He specialized in Arachnology. What kind of man takes the scariest things on the planet and studies them? I grew up wrapped in the eight greasy hairy legs of his dreams and have had nothing but the upmost resentment for spiders. Spiders were everywhere. They were in cages, collages, coffee mugs, and wallpaper. He used to wake me up in the middle of the night and tell me not to move because one of the world's most poisonous spiders happened to be taking a nap on my face. By the time I was seven years old I had been bitten by almost every spider in his precious catalogue. But it wasn't until my mother died that I began to really hate them.

I came home from school to find all the lights on and food burning in the kitchen. I was ten years old, and although I knew how to use the stove I knew better than to touch it. It was not like my mom to leave the stove going, and it was not like her to burn food either. I walked past the kitchen and saw a light on in the bathroom. As I slowly opened the door steam began to hit my face. The shower was running. It had been set to a timer and it would come on for thirty minutes every two hours. The downstairs bathroom was an off limits place for me.

The Sydney Funnel-web Spider is one of the most toxic spiders to humans. Although it was small it could easily kill a small human and especially a boy like me. To keep the spider safe, my father kept it in the downstairs bathroom and a timer on the shower to keep the humidity at the right levels so it wouldn't try to escape. My father knew best.

My mother was lying on the floor and the spider was nowhere to be seen. The paramedics would later tell me that she had already been dead for about four hours. I ran to her and tried to shake her. I rolled her over and webs were spun across her open eyes. The spider was hiding underneath her and when it felt threatened it sprung and bit me on the hand. I blacked out.

My father was in tears when the paramedics rolled my mother out. He wasn't crying for her though. His favorite pet project had been killed and what was left of it was being held and cried on. They say I killed it but I don't remember. The same bite that killed my mother left some dead nerves in my right hand but I was still alive. All those bites my father allowed to happen apparently aided to my toxicity. I should probably thank him, but I might as well be dead. He never looked me in the eyes again.

Fast forward to when I was sixteen and the first time he tried to kill me on purpose. He bought me a car for my birthday. A normal person would have put a bomb in it. My dad puts a family of brown recluse spiders under the seat. Lucky for me I expected this sort of behavior and immediately sold the car to a friend for a date with his girlfriend, who upon his death became my girlfriend. Thanks dad.

The next and last attempt at my life came when I was eighteen. He had been spending most of his time in the basement mixing spider genes together to try and create venom toxic enough to kill me. I'm surprised it only took two years. He told me to come down to the basement and that he wanted to show me something. I took a box of matches and a small bottle of lighter fluid with me. The basement barbeque was the last time I saw my dad. I read in the paper that he survived with mild burns, but I know that it was the graduation party of the year, and both of us would never forget it.

Now, back to the man in the box, who doesn't know he is on camera. I broke into the house and slipped him about five Valiums in his food. After he went down I began to dig. I dug right into the floor of the basement. The foundation broke and the blackest dirt you have ever seen spilled through. Once I got to the depth I wanted I began the construction on the box. I installed sixteen cameras in various angles and then set it into the hole. Next I began my favorite part of the plan. I laid my father on the table and began to cut into his eye. I popped his right eye out and let it hang across his face. Then I got the briefcase out of my car. I have been working on this for about six months. The egg sack was about a day away from hatching over a hundred baby spiders, and I placed it in my father's empty eye socket. Then I stuffed his eye back in his head and stitched it closed. I threw him the six feet into his coffin and shut the lid. I didn't begin to smile until the sound of dirt hitting his coffin became the only thing I could hear.

My father slept for another thirteen hours. I spent the time looking through family photos and talking to his unconscious face on the screen. I told him that I finally remembered what happened the day my mother was killed. I told him that after the bite on my hand that I grabbed the spider and pinned it to the floor just like he taught me. I used my thumbs to trace the spider's knuckles and bent each leg backward until it snapped off. I told him that I remembered the unique way a spider screams and that his favorite pet screamed after every single one of his eight legs was ripped off. Next I told him that I took the torso back to the kitchen and emptied the skillet of burned food on to the floor and threw the spider into the hot pan and watched it squirm until it stopped moving. Then I put it on a plate, set the table for all three of us and sat down waiting for him to get home. I told him that I remembered what he said to me when he got home and that it was time for him to be reunited with his family.

My father stirred. He began mumbling and slowly moving his fingers. Then he spent some time doing the "I can't believe I'm buried alive thing" which we both know was only for attention. I tried to ignore him, but at this point I wasn't just smiling, I was laughing. He suddenly stopped and put his hand to his eye. It was apparently show time. I moved the cameras to get the perfect angle and zoomed in. I want to see the look on his face when he finally gets it, when he finally realizes that it was me that did it to him, when he finally realizes that he won't be getting out of this alive. He began to scream. I will never forget the look on his face.

His teeth looked so white in the dark as his silent screams filled the screen. The eggs should be hatching anytime now, and when they do, they will begin to eat his eye from the inside and slowly make their way out to his face and the rest of him. He pulled back his hand and it was covered in blood. He tried to pull his own eye out, beautiful. Well he got it half way out. I guess that should be something he should have been proud of. Blood began pouring down his face and he held one little finger up to get a better view. There was the tiniest spider crawling on his index finger, the first to break free.

He knew it. He knew everything. He knew that soon there would be hundreds of them and that they would come pouring out of his eye eating him alive. He began to look frantically around the box and stopped on one of the cameras. He looked right into my eyes and mouthed my name...

I left him to die with his family.

Love Never Screams

She told me her name was Lucie. She was my Lucie. I first met her from afar. I stole casual glances from street corners and through windows, never allowing myself to be seen. I made up stories about her life with me. We would grow old on a swinging timeline never losing sight of one another. And we could never die.

I watched her for a solid six months. I spent my days observing her schedule, and memorizing her routines. In the mornings she would pick flowers that grew in the cracks of the sidewalks. I could never understand why she didn't just trample them like everyone else, and I never wanted to be a flower more in my entire life.

She wore pink shoes, and wherever she went she made sure to smile and pet every dog that crossed her path. She was beautiful. She worked outside of a bakery giving away free samples of danishes and cinnamon rolls to strangers. I knew she was special because she never talked to any of the guys that came up to her. She would just shrug and give them a sample. I wanted to talk to her so bad, but the timing just wasn't right.

After work she would walk through the park on her way home. I followed her every day at a twenty second pace. She never knew I was behind her trying to count every strand of her hair. Every night I would start over and try to count them all before she got home. Her home was small, but comfortable looking, and she lived alone at such a young age. She must have been very mature and responsible. She would read every night just before sundown, and I would watch her fall asleep. As thoughts of her flooded my mind I would fall asleep to the sight of her sleeping outline under a mound of blankets.

I began to prepare for our first meeting. The morning started out the usual way. I walked behind her watching her picking all the flowers in the sidewalk and petting every dog. You could feel her smile light the city like a fusion reaction. When she was in sight people said, "What sun?". We walked to her work together and when she walked in to get her samples I just kept on going. I rounded the corner and took off at a sprint to the opposite side of the street and doubled back just in time to watch her come out with her tray. As the day went on I kept running through all the scenarios that might happen when I finally talk to her. Would she laugh? Would she smile? Would she like me?

Finally her shift was over and we began the long walk back to her home with me still trying to count her strands of hair, until the unthinkable happened. She looked over her shoulder and actually saw me. I kept it cool and just kept walking, but then she did it again. She started walking faster and it became more difficult to count her hair so I started walking faster. A few seconds later she broke into a run. I started to chase her. I couldn't let her get away. I chased her all the way to her bed and she jumped under the blankets trying to hide. I drew close knowing that familiar form in that mound of blankets and drew out a knife. I knew she couldn't love me, couldn't ever love me. Without her smile there was no sunlight, and if she wanted darkness then baby, darkness was what I had most. I stabbed her. I stabbed her so many times the blankets began to fall apart into little bloody cotton shapes. I stood back looking at the mess that was once my Lucie. I peeled back layer after layer of blood soaked cloth until I finally saw her face. It was contorted into this screaming ugly mask that was not the Lucie I loved. Not my Lucie.

She never screamed. Maybe she did love me after all because not once did she scream. The world was darker, I was darker. I would do anything to have her light in my life again. I reached into my pocket and brought out a pack of matches and a small bottle of paint thinner. I poured the liquid over my love and struck the blaze hot. The light, my light, my Lucie, was warming my world again.

After the embers died down all that was left was her ashes and a few resilient bones. I began scraping them up into a big pile in my hands and started singing to them. After a short song I took a bite, then another. After each dirty mouthful I shed a tear and yet I could not stop eating her ashes. Her ashes warm and grainy weighed heavy on my heart and stomach. My Lucie, she said her name was Lucie.

Missing Persons Police Report:

Missing
Laura- Age 13, Pink Shoes
Deaf
Known to Sleep in Alleys
Last Seen in Front of Donut Shop
If Seen Please Contact Local Authorities
Suspected Foul Play

Eating For Two

The secret, as anybody will tell you, is low heat and long hours. The meat will fall straight off the bones, and you can almost taste the time baked into it. Sweet succulent nourishment fills the room like a storm of aroma. It is my favorite meal, and I am going to tell you how to prepare it.

First off, we need the ingredients:

1 Chicken (preferably young)

1 bag of potatoes unpeeled

1 box of stuffing mix

1 c. Jack Daniels

Ground Pepper (to taste)

1 grapefruit

Now, I'm going to give you a few pointers on how to pick a ripe chicken. When I do my shopping, I pick some place like a super market or a mall play center. Some place that a young chicken will easily get separated from its mother and run to any kind looking adult for guidance. The right age for a good eating chicken is 18 months old. If the mothers refuse to use years instead of months then why should I? This is the best age because it is during this time of development that muscle begins to replace fat, and growth is the most important task of the body. Also, it doesn't hurt that no one besides their mothers can understand what the hell they are saying.

Another important note is when you pick your chicken, try to keep in mind these simple letters: FTHR. Fat to height ratio is important when trying to understand the tenderness of your chicken, along with the flexibility of meal planning. Try not to pick the one who is constantly jumping, screaming, or swinging from the monkey bars. You really want the sad fucker in the sand box who is oblivious to the world.

Now that you have picked a chicken and got it home, you can start the marinade. I like to take the cup of Jack Daniels and put it in a bottle. Chickens at this age should be able to hold a bottle on their own, but when it is full of liquor they may need a little bit of help. Duck tape will help even the most resistant chickens to drink all of their milk. This accomplishes two tasks. The first is, your chicken will now take a nap and be less resistant. The second is that by the time the body heats up, all that liquor should be processing through his liver and be forced out of his pores, coating your entire meal with a smoky Kentucky backwoods type flavor. Yum.

I don't peel potatoes. The skin, like most of the food I eat, is the best part. There is a level of crunch involved. A charred blackened layer of goodness is on every bite, and my potatoes are no exception. So I simply cut them into chunks and line the pan with them. I make a nice comfy bed for our chicken to take a nap in while I prepare the rest of the meal. I make the stuffing and pad it onto the chicken like a nice little blanket, making sure to tuck him in, and then I add the ground pepper and squeeze the grapefruit over the whole thing.

You want to set your oven at 250 degrees and bake for about eight hours. You can tell when it is done when all the little hairs are burned off of the chicken, even the little eyelashes. The skin should be dark but not burned, and every bite should be a little bit crispy. Serve hot, and eat plenty, after all, you are eating for two.

Sh...Sh...IREN

I have had this song stuck in my head, my hands, my heart for almost three days. It drowns everything out. Most of the time, I am not even sure if I am still breathing. In fact, I am not sure if I have ever taken a breath before now. This should have been top priority. After all, there is a difference between not needing to breathe and holding one's breath. However, when an obsession takes hold of your world, it is not hard to walk that line, and more often than not, I can't remember which side my allegiance falls on.

Waves crash, gulls call, and I hold my breath listening deeply, all the way to the marrow. Heavy clouds line the horizon and the sun may or may not have been seen for years. It took three days for the discovery. The sudden understanding struck me like lightening from an Edison bow. Although the song was inside me, behind my eyes, circulating my body, it did not originate from me.

My first salty kiss from my forever lover stings with a ferocity rarely seen. The ocean, it seems, is perfect. It gives and takes, as I flounder.

The cold, menacing with its embrace, loves me more than I could ever know. It makes men hard, and weak in one breath. It clings to me, offering obstacle and reward, and I press on. The song, louder now, ringing in my everything, as I venture further and further down.

A crushing weight begins in my ears, spreading slowly to my eyes. They both protest bursting and refuse to go any further. Darkness consumes me. Either the star is out of reach, or I have simply closed my eyes in an attempt to keep them in my head. I am not sure which is true. All I know is the song is louder than ever.

I feel it in my teeth, vibrating like an ancient language of the sea. My tongue is several sizes too big, and the thought of whale crosses my mind. I maintain the image of using my tongue as a floatation device for what feels like several hours, but I most likely made that up.

My fingers no longer have skin, if in fact, they had skin to begin with. Skinny breaking bones grasp the bottom and feel the beating of the song like a pulse that once accompanied them. I grasp a handle, and as I do, my eyes open. It is made of glass, and very old, but it is singing to me like a friend I once knew. No, like a mistreated lover that once owned my heart. Sinister, like me, it feels deeply, and moves with me.

The glass bottle is upside down, and mostly full of water and sediment. I pick it up, turning it softly on beat with the song. It has a cork and as I turn it, small refugee bubbles begin to trickle out. It is now that the question of breath comes to me. My lungs, like storms, long ago embraced the calm after the hell, and have not since made a single attempt to recover. But at the sight of the bubbles, something stirs in me. I can no longer see the surface of the water, and for the first time, the thought of a return trip, with my prize, crosses my mind.

The song changes tempo. My head, my hands, my heart begin to race. I burn like love in an open wound, and swim towards the up.

Sunlight, warming and inviting in a sea of grey, begins to illuminate my surroundings. I see current, and time. Both seem to be dying. My sight, tunneled and red, begins to fail. I cling to my prize and revel in the thought of being together forever.

As I begin to float, my vision gone, my hands change key. The song begins to crash out of tune and waves become long. The cork sinks, and with the bottle to my lips, I breathe. I kick and breach with the bottle high in my hands, while half of the ocean pours from my guts. My eyes are reborn, and with a new soul, I can finally see the world. I am clean. I look into the bottle looking for my prize, but the song is sung, and the light quickly fades. Darkness blankets the sky and the waves begin to thrash. There is no land in sight and out of the depth a song begins to grow louder, as I realize that it really was in me all along.

Printed in the USA
CPSIA information can be obtained
at www.ICGtesting.com
LVHW091334191023
761544LV00001B/219